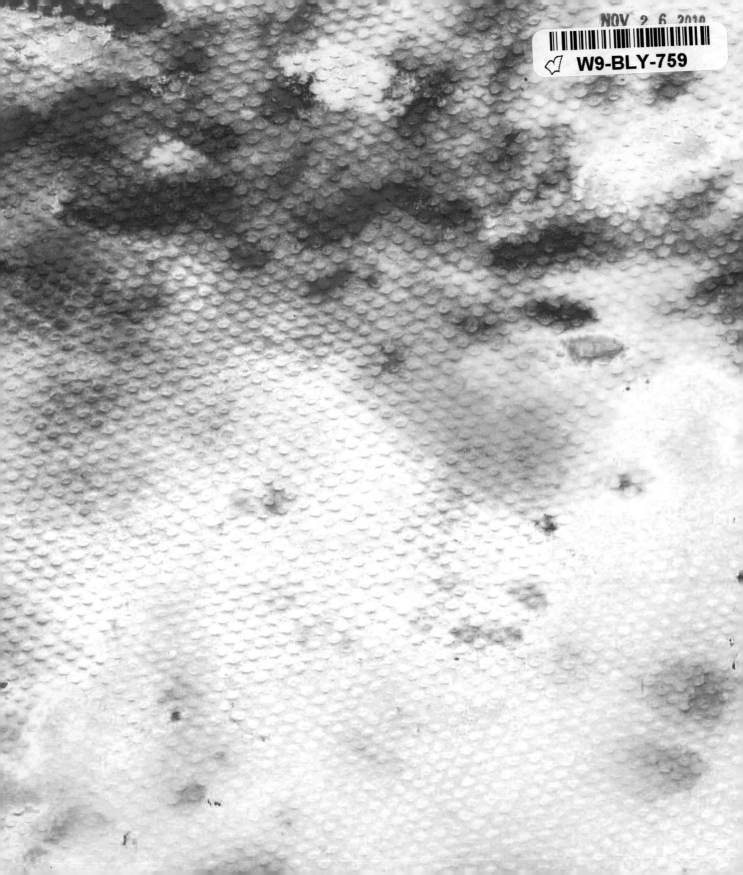

NOV 2 6 2019

W9-BLY-759

ALSO BY MARK Z. DANIELEWSKI

House of Leaves

Only Revolutions

The Fifty Year Sword

The Familiar (Volumes 1 – 5)

Mark Z. Danielewski's

CHARLESTON COUNTY LIBRARY

The Little Blue Kite

Pantheon Books, New York

WITHDRAWN

The Little Blue Kite

NAMES, CHARACTERS, PLACES, AND INCIDENTS, AS WELL AS CLOUDS, BREEZES, AND FEARS, AND CERTAINLY KITES OF ALL SHAPES, SIZES, AND HUES RISE OUT OF THE AUTHOR'S IMAGINATION. THIS IS AFTER ALL A WORK OF FICTION. AND BECAUSE FICTION'S PROVINCE IS THE IMAGINATION AND THUS CONCERNED WITH THE ARGUMENT OF EMPATHY OVER REPRESENTATION, ANY RESEMBLANCE TO ACTUAL PERSONS, LIVING OR DEAD, EVENTS, OR LOCALES, NO MATTER HOW STRANGE OR FAMILIAR, DISTANT OR CLOSE, SHOULD BE CONSIDERED COINCIDENCES BORN OUT OF THE READERS' KEEN AND EXPANSIVE MIND.

Copyright © 2019 by Mark Z. Danielewski

All rights reserved. Published in the United States by Pantheon Books, a division of Penguin Random House LLC, New York, and distributed in Canada by Penguin Random House Canada Limited, Toronto.

Pantheon Books and colophon are registered trademarks of Penguin Random House LLC.

Library of Congress Cataloging-in-Publication Data

Danielewski, Mark Z.
The Little Blue Kite / Mark Z. Danielewski.
Description: First edition. New York: Pantheon Books, 2019.
Identifiers: LCCN 2019004445.
ISBN 9781524747695 (hardcover: alk. paper).
ISBN 9781524747701 (ebook).
Subjects: LCSH: Graphic novels.
Classification: LCC PN6727.D2626 L58 2019
DDC 741.5/973—dc23
LC record available at lccn.loc.gov/2019004445

Jacket and Case by Atelier Z.

Fonts: Dante (Title & Author), *Apollo* (©), Legacy (Dedication), *Transitional (Epigraph)*, Bliss (JP et al.), Tempus (Folios), *and* Gilgamesh (Credits).

Before Dark's unfettered name,
beyond VEM's untroubled gaze,
tomorrow's gate waits unlatched.
Remember: Whim's candle needs no flame
— her Art outdoes every blaze.
No strings attached.

Printed in Canada

First Edition
2 4 6 8 9 7 5 3 1

markzdanielewski.com
pantheonbooks.com

For Ms. Cooper, my high school biology teacher, who taught me that there is a world beyond this world and it is still this world . . .

The great sky is open.

— Mumon Ekai

In a closet lives a little blue kite.

8

It isn't even put together. It lives in pieces at the bottom of a brown paper bag at the back of a closet without a light.

Once upon a time there was another kite.

It wasn't in a paper bag let alone in a closet.

And it certainly wasn't in pieces.

It was a very put-together kite of spectacular color.

Little Kai loved this kite.

Little Kai flew this kite so much its newness quickly faded. Branches of majestic trees tore the fabric. Kai lost count of how many times this kite smacked into the ground. Once so hard the spine splintered.

Again and again, little Kai would sit cross-legged on the floor, repairing each rip and fracture with Band-Aids and safety pins.

The handle was shaped like an *O* and wrapped with thread from an enormous spider! Really, it was Kai's bighearted but very tiny grandmother who had gently attached the silk thread to that spectacular kite and told him to keep flying higher and higher until no thread was left.

"Then you might reach the edge of the Murk."

"But Grandma," little Kai had cried, "I don't want to reach the edge of the Murk! I want to escape the Murk!"

Now what, you might ask, is the Murk?

The Murk has been around for a long, long time. And it affects everyone. Some are blinded by it, others blind to it, while a few — if rumors are true — have escaped it entirely.

In the Murk you feel surrounded, bound up, and even on the clearest day, buried in a haze.

As if you were drowning but still just able to breathe.

No bars mark the Murk but all around is a cage.

Unfortunately, with not even half the thread flung skyward, Kai's spectacular kite was almost out of sight, and yet, as little Kai discovered, that still wasn't high enough to reach even the edge of the Murk.

But Kai never quit, again and again releasing more and more loops, **until one day an awful thing happened:**

 a great roar split the sky and the thread . . . snapped.

For little Kai it was as if an immense monster too immense for any one name and hungrier than all the emptiness that haunts the space between all the stars **had devoured his spectacular kite.**

Not one   itty-bitty   shred survived.

Kai just stood   there   alone   on the grass,
breathless, with   the Murk   swirling   in   thicker
than ever   before,   until   he   couldn't
make   sense   of his   feet let alone
the sky   even   though   his feet were
                      right there   and   the sky was all
around.

Kai had never felt   so devastated.

To lose that kite was to lose joy itself.
Which was like losing himself.

Because isn't in joy when we feel most ourselves?

That feeling of joy was the closest little Kai
had ever come to being murkless.

15

Not long after losing that spectacular kite, little Kai lost all his friends too. You see, his family was forced to move to a new place, where Kai was a stranger to everyone he met.

Fortunately, at his new school, Kai had a teacher he liked very much. She had hair bold as silver and eyes bright as green breaking waves. She seemed to understand him better than anyone else.

Her name was Joy Penseons.

Whenever little Kai got so excited that he couldn't finish anything or when he felt so devoured by doubt that he couldn't start anything, Ms. Penseons would demonstrate how to listen to every breath in order to relax.

One day, on one particularly gray afternoon, when little Kai was both too excited and too doubtful to do much of anything, except maybe cry, **Ms. Penseons asked Kai to stay after class.**

"Cultivate gentle thoughts and calm the sky of your mind," she suggested.

Kai, though, was not so easily pacified and blurted back: "What is that supposed to mean? 'Gentle thoughts'? 'Sky of your mind'? How can a thought be gentle?!"

If Kai expected Ms. Penseons to get cross, her delight surprised him. "Excellent questions, Kai! But first answer me this: if your mind is not a sky, what is it?"

Little Kai tried to picture his mind but all he saw was a jumble of thoughts that looked like big knots bulging all over a very old tree. Which Kai tried to describe to Ms. Penseons.

Ms. Penseons looked pleased. "Now, what if, instead, those thoughts were, well, light as birds and bright as air?"

"For one thing, they wouldn't look like knots on a very old tree."

"Wonderful! Now tell me quick: what do you see without that tree?" And Ms. Penseons planted both her elbows on her desk and rested her chin in the cradle of her hands, like she was about to hear the most fabulous story.

But little Kai just shook his head. He didn't know what a mind might look like that was light as a bird and bright as air.

"Could it look like a sky?" Ms. Penseons suggested with a wink.

"Maybe." Which was the best Kai could do because just trying to picture a sky made up of thoughts that were so light and bright that maybe they weren't thoughts at all made his head knot up with thoughts far heavier than big bulging knots on a very old tree, until the way he saw everything grew very dark and even terrifying, which he didn't share with Ms. Penseons.

Instead, he asked her: "Is that what you mean by gentle thoughts?"

How Ms. Penseons smiled then! It was a smile so big it was easily bigger than every great fear is finally very, very small.

"Very impressive, Kai! The more gentle your thoughts, the more open your sky. How else then, well, to do Good?" Which little Kai didn't understand at all, but before he could answer her question with his own question, **Ms. Penseons reached beneath her desk and took out a brown paper bag.**

Kai peered inside and oh how his eyes widened when he saw The Little Blue Kite! Even if it was in pieces at the bottom.

He wanted to take it out at once but Ms. Penseons stayed his eagerness with a soft hand.

"Only fly it . . . well, when you're ready."

"Ready for what?"

"To be you."

Kai never saw Ms. Penseons again nor did he ever find out what happened to her. The next day she was just gone.

And then for the second time in Kai's young life, there appeared that immense monster too immense for any one name and hungrier than all the emptiness that haunts the space between all the stars. Only this time, instead of a kite, it had devoured Ms. Penseons!

Little Kai was so sad, he didn't even want to go flying.

So you know what he did?

Kai just shoved that brown paper bag
to the back of his closet
without a light.

Weeks slipped by until weeks became months and eventually months became years. Kai left behind childhood and tried to welcome adulthood, which he soon discovered was very busy. There was just so much to do. So much so that there was hardly time to think about a closet, let alone a brown paper bag, let alone what waited inside.

Some might have sworn that Kai had forgotten The Little Blue Kite altogether.

But they would have been wrong.

Now, before we get to Kai's great adventure, let's see how he's doing all grown up.

First and foremost, Kai has never forgotten Ms. Penseons's advice, and to this day works hard at having gentle thoughts, even if he's still unsure what a gentle thought really is.

Second, **Kai is very kind.** In fact, if you happened to meet Kai — and how lucky you would be! — he would likely open the door for you, or help you with something you dropped, or wish you a pleasant day even if it was cold and overcast. Kai knows how to have a pleasant day even if it is cold and overcast.

Kai often surprises his family with flowers, lemon cake, or a black-and-white box filled with figs, for no particular reason either, except that **Kai loves his family. And Kai's family loves him.** They love his honesty, his loyalty, and, of course, his compassion. They love having him around as much as possible.

Kai's friends love him in much the same way. They praise his generosity and are grateful when he helps them through their heartaches. Kai's employers at the company where he designs games are equally enthusiastic, commending Kai's devotion and hard work. Strangers too can tell that Kai is very good and very, very brave. Because, as Ms. Penseons would surely have agreed: how can you be good if you're not brave?

But Kai has a secret! Only he knows just how scared the thought of flying The Little Blue Kite makes him!

How awful is that! Can you even imagine?! To be most frightened of what you most adore! It almost sounds too strange to believe.

True, now and then Kai cracks open that closet, if only to just as quickly slam the door tight.

That is, until today . . .

Today, it turns out, is a special day.

And no, not because it's a holiday or birthday. You certainly won't find this day marked on anyone's calendar. Kai isn't even feeling that great, though he isn't feeling so bad either.

The most important thing about this particular day is that Kai has a little extra time. Extra time is a curious thing. No one really knows how extra time comes around, but in Kai's case it might have a lot to do with a wind rising in a deep sky that is not too wild yet not too mild.

Make no mistake: like everyone else, Kai has many distractions, but one advantage of endeavoring to have gentle thoughts is that distractions are no longer important enough to do away with extra time.

When Kai gets home, he hurries straight to that closet. His family is sure surprised to see him hurrying so but they are even more surprised to discover a closet in their home that no one had noticed before.

Kai throws open the closet door and scoops up the brown paper bag.

The sight of The Little Blue Kite inside takes Kai's breath away and blurs his eyes, though Kai can't say why for sure.

The same is true for The Little Blue Kite.

Very gently, Kai lays out all the parts on the floor. Then he spreads wide the fabric, which he calls a sail, and inserts the spine. Finally, he unfolds the long blue tail.

Only when Kai gets to the handle shaped like a big *B,* which was once upon a time carved out of the wood of a fallen ash tree and later spooled with countless loops of the finest silvery thread . . . only then does Kai pause.

One end of the thread is lost at the heart of that big *B* while the other end dangles free, ready to be tied to the sail.

But oh how just that loose end overwhelms Kai. He at once remembers his two greatest losses — his kite of spectacular color and, of course, the disappearance of Ms. Penseons.

Kai has to step away, leaving The Little Blue Kite just lying there, unassembled, unfinished, abandoned on the floor.

Now, I expect some of you might snicker at Kai's silly and, well, yes, perhaps exaggerated reactions to a little blue kite. But let's agree that snickering isn't nice, especially when it concerns someone else's fear.

After all, who hasn't in the grip of fear felt certain that their fear was beyond questioning — whether it concerned, say, a fragile daddy longlegs weaving a messy net, or apprehension before a crowd of openhearted folks waiting to hear you speak, or how the dread of a dark closet might make you avoid altogether certain hallways in your house? And this last fear can go very deep, because there are so many different types of closets.

We have all fallen prey to fear, even if all our fears look different, especially the little ones, and when it comes to big fears, like, for example, an immense monster too immense for any one name, how can we begin to face that if we can't handle the little ones?

Anyway, quite a few days pass after Kai's first attempt at assembling The Little Blue Kite.

Storms arrive, too dangerous for flying, followed by quiet days too still for flying.

Until one day, the deep sky offers up yet another afternoon of mild, perfectly welcoming wind.

Kai's heart leaps. Ever since freeing The Little Blue Kite from the closet, he has thought of nothing else but flying and even escaping the Murk.

So Kai takes a deep breath, gets down on his knees, and attaches the thread with a simple knot. But already he's unsure whether something so simple can suffice. So Kai ties as many knots as there are in his stomach.

Then Kai carries The Little Blue Kite to a clearing he likes. He sets The Little Blue Kite on the ground, lays out the long blue tail, and then, after fiercely gripping the wooden handle, unwinds a few loops of silvery thread.

Immediately, panic seizes his chest and strangles his breath.

It makes no difference that birds joy the sky.

Kai not only reloops the thread back around the handle but **returns The Little Blue Kite to the back of that closet without a light,** making sure to shut the door tight.

More time slips away **but Kai never forgets The Little Blue Kite.**

And somehow . . .
The Little Blue Kite knows this too.

Until one afternoon, a bright azure sky calls to Kai with strong summer breezes and clouds scudding by without the burden of rain.

Again, **Kai returns to the clearing.** Again, he unwinds several loops of silvery thread. This time, though, with hardly a tug, **Kai lofts up The Little Blue Kite.** He doesn't even need a quick backward skip.

The wind just takes hold.

True, The Little Blue Kite isn't so high.

It isn't so far away either, but it is indeed flying.

And what joy finds **Kai!**

At long last, The Little Blue Kite is free of its closet and Kai is smiling and oh how the deep sky beckons! Even the Murk seems to lessen a tiny bit. So Kai lets out a little more thread, only to stop short. You see, The Little Blue Kite has started shaking so wildly back and forth that it seems to be shouting —

No!

No!

No!

No more!

No higher!

Please bring me down now!

Which Kai does at once.

In the days that follow, Kai continues to return to his clearing even if without fail The Little Blue Kite continues to shake in the slow wind —

No!   No!   No!

— and ever more desperately too, especially when Kai dares to release yet another silvery loop of thread before frantically changing his mind and, fast as fast can, drags The Little Blue Kite back down to his trembling hands.

But Kai never gives up and each time manages to fly The Little Blue Kite, well, a tiny bit higher.

Now and then The Little Blue Kite even flies steady.

Sometimes it almost seems calm.

Though never Kai.

Only one thing makes his fear bearable:

Kai always flies

The Little Blue Kite

very low.

We should point out here that Kai's new preoccupation has not gone unnoticed.

"Why are you spending so much time by yourself?" his family complains.

"You're being so weird!" his friends criticize.

"What do you mean 'me-time'?" his employers object.

Kai suggests that perhaps they too should try flying little kites. To which all of them reply:

"Are you kidding?! Who has extra time for that?!"

Their dismissals hurt but Kai recognizes that great adventures often start in ways that those closest to you   can't commend and those you don't know won't even try   to comprehend. Besides —

Kai just loves flying The Little Blue Kite.
And the more he flies, the deeper in love he falls.

And so summer goes, and with autumn's dying leaves bright against the coming cold, Kai keeps returning to his clearing, each time flying The Little Blue Kite a little bit higher, even as the fear of losing everything never ceases to race his heart.

If someone in Kai's family or one of Kai's friends or a stranger had asked why he persisted with this solitary pursuit, Kai might have mumbled something about escaping the Murk and even wistfully added in an awfully inconclusive way:

"I believe — though I don't know exactly how it is that I believe this — that here is a way to do good on behalf of those I know well, those I've just met, those I'll someday meet, and those I'll never meet. Here is even a way to do good on behalf of those that time tells us are gone."

"Do good?" might be the follow-up question. "By flying a silly little blue kite?"

Kai never stops freeing more and more silvery thread, and though still buried deep within the Murk, **The Little Blue Kite finally does manage to fly as high as a very tall evergreen. Though no higher.**

Kai, you see, has reached his limit.

Maybe you've experienced something similar, like an unwillingness to pedal any faster as you race your bike down a steep hill or dive deep enough to touch the bottom of a lake or climb one rung higher on a very tall ladder.

Except when Kai realizes this — that he's stuck — he screws up his courage and frees one more loop.

Immediately, The Little Blue Kite jumps to a height surpassing the tallest forests the world over.

Unfortunately, this small victory comes at a steep price:

**The Little Blue Kite shakes so violently
as if not only to shout but this time
scream —**

No!
No!
No!

No more!

No higher!

Please bring me down now!

How Kai's hands clench then! How his arms ache! Awful cramps chomp at his neck as knots big as bulging knots on a very old tree twist into his spine.

Kai almost gives up. But then he remembers his old teacher Ms. Penseons, and just the thought of her quiets his heart.

Kai even hears her voice:

"Cultivate gentle thoughts and calm the sky of your mind."

The wind, though, doesn't quiet, growing stronger and louder and ever more dangerous, which makes Kai want to cry and drag The Little Blue Kite out of the sky.

Kai's fear escalates so quickly then that he's sure the thread will snap.

Even the wooden handle shaped like a big *B* seems ready to slip from his grasp because fright has made Kai's palms wet with sweat and his fingers prickle so badly that he can barely feel anything anymore.

Except the thread is true and doesn't snap.

And Kai's hold is true and the handle doesn't slip.

And then Kai does something very surprising.

Can you guess what?

Remember, Kai is very, very brave.

Kai lets out a little more thread!

That's right!

And then he lets out still more thread!

In fact, Kai lets out more thread than ever before!

Whereupon something quite amazing takes place:

The Little Blue Kite still keeps shaking
but this time it's not to cry out —

No!

No!

No!

No more!

No higher!

Please bring me down now!

but rather —

No!

No!

No!

Not lower!

Not down there!

Higher, higher please!

You might say The Little Blue Kite even tilts
this way and that way with glee.

And Kai keeps releasing   more and more thread.

And The Little Blue   Kite keeps rising higher and higher, past bars of
sunlight, mists of   winter gray, and beams of air so dark, they seem
kissed by night, even   though it's the middle of the day.

Nor does The Little Blue Kite stop there.

Up through roaring winds...

Up through dangerous winds...
and all the warring winds that haunt the places
where power reigns until power too fails.

Until Kai has unwound the whole spool!

Or *almost* unwound the whole spool.

One last loop remains.

And what's more, it's not attached to that handle shaped like a big *B*. It's not attached to anything . . .

Only Kai doesn't notice this! Kai just keeps struggling to see The Little Blue Kite, which is so high that not even squinting really helps.

drop that handle shaped like a big B and snatch hold of the end.

And so when Kai frees the last loop, the thread just slips away . . . and would have escaped too, if Kai didn't, fast as fast can,

Poor Kai just wants to drag The Little Blue Kite down out of the sky.

And why shouldn't he?

What else can he do?

What would you do?

And the worst part? The Little Blue Kite still hasn't escaped the Murk. The Little Blue Kite hasn't even reached the edge of the Murk.

"Maybe I've been wrong all along," Kai confesses to the Murk — for who else is there to confess to now? "Maybe this was never a great adventure. Maybe this too, like some silly game, was just another dumb distraction."

Even if Kai has also started to feel something he's never felt before: it's as if the thread Kai holds wants to let go of him!

Which is when Kai at last understands:

the time has come for

The Little Blue Kite

to fly on.

Kai's heart stops beating so fast.

In fact, Kai's heart just breaks.

Whereupon the Murk grows so thick that Kai can't see his feet, let alone the sky, even though his feet are right there and the sky is all around.

But because Kai loves The Little Blue Kite so much . . .

Kai lets go.

Now, who on earth would dream of doing that?

Not that Kai even thinks twice about what he didn't think once about, because the strangest thing of all just took place:

when Kai let go of the thread,

it wasn't The Little Blue Kite that

flew away . . .

it was Kai!

You see, Kai

— much more than he is Kai —

has all along been

The Little Blue Kite too!

But you already knew that, didn't you?

How fast does

Kai

The Little Blue Kite rise!

Away
Kai
The Little Blue Kite flies!

Higher than never before!

Far beyond the Murk!

Free!

Kai
The Little Blue Kite flies over immense cities
and slumbering towns.

Kai
**The Little Blue Kite flies over great jungles
and towering mountains.**

Kai
The Little Blue Kite flies over burning sands and melting ice.

Kai

The Little Blue Kite flies over oceans wild with cyclones.

Kai The Little Blue Kite flies over seas so glassy,
they dare the moon to know itself as only a reflection.
Years and years race by, or so it seems,
followed by yet another lifetime of years,
until

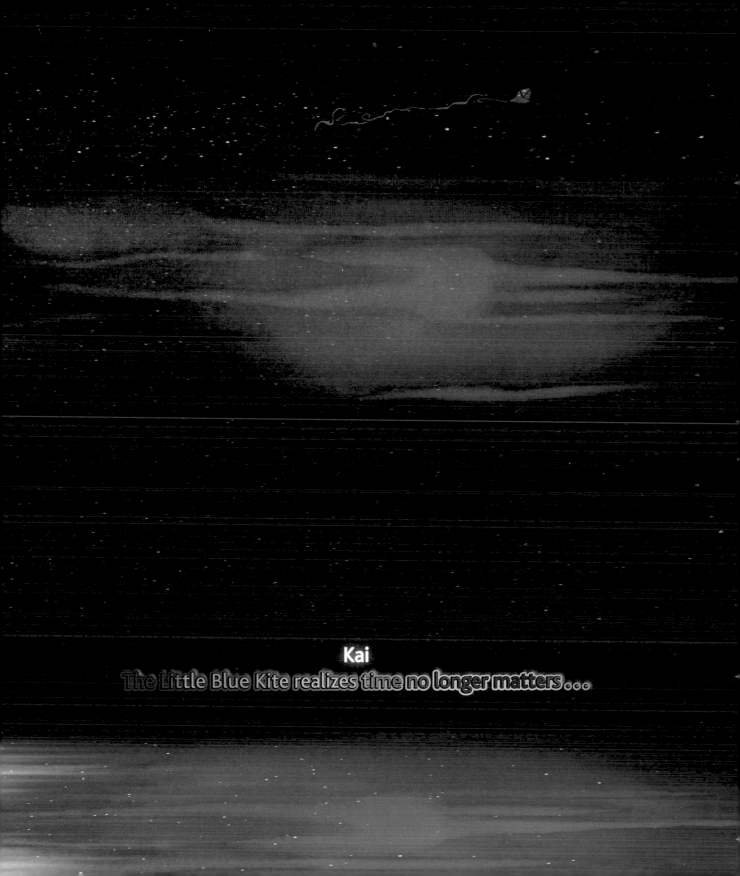

Kai

The Little Blue Kite realizes time no longer matters . . .

Then Kai The Little Blue Kite wonders: "What use is this thread I keep trailing behind me?"

And when no answer comes, Kai The Little Blue Kite undoes the many knots he once tied a long, long time ago and releases the thread.

Because Kai The Little Blue Kite still holds the long blue tail, he continues to fly straight — as if heading certainly toward a distant coast or a star burning bright.

Except because Kai The Little Blue Kite is not heading toward a distant coast or heeding any heavenly direction, **Kai The Little Blue Kite even lets go of the tail.**

How Kai The Little Blue Kite goes spinning then!

Back around!

Upside down!

upside down!

and back around means

downs mean right-side up,

Until so many upside

And so it goes that right-side up matters no more than coming back around no longer matters, because when you're no longer going someplace, you can let go of left and you can let go of right and you can let go of up and you can let go of down in the same way that you can let go altogether of . . . direction.

Which is what Kai The Little Blue Kite does next!

Kai The Little Blue Kite lets go of direction!

Now, how is any of that possible?

Well, that's a very good question.

And it's a question that Kai The Little Blue Kite also asks,
and oh how quickly the Murk returns!

And even worse, **out of nowhere comes an awful roar!**
So hungry it swallows its own roar before
its own roar can even start!

How Kai cowers in fear!
Before such harrowing silence!

And who can blame him?

Behold!

A terror so complete nothing
challenges its dominion!

Behold what no living thing
will ever survive!

The Immense Monster Too
Immense for Any One Name
and Hungrier Than All
the Emptiness That
Haunts the Space
Between All
the Stars!

And so Kai The Little Blue Kite just falls . . .

a

long

and

terrible

tumbling

down

and

down . . .

Until all Kai The Little Blue Kite can think to do is miss his good family, and his good friends, and all the good strangers he now and then used to meet.

Kai The Little Blue Kite even misses Kai with his aching fist — the one that once gripped so fiercely a handle shaped like a big *B* wound up with so much silvery thread no longer his to hold.

But most of all, Kai The Little Blue Kite misses his favorite teacher, Ms. Penseons. He misses her hair bold as silver and eyes bright as green breaking waves. Which is when Kai realizes something that was never his to realize before: after flying so much, Kai's thoughts are no longer like big bulging knots on an old fallen tree. Instead, they are light as birds and bright as air.

Kai's mind is wide open! Kai's mind has become a sky!

And suddenly there is so much room!

Not only for birds rejoicing a breeze! Or thundershowers and coyotes and peacocks and raccoons back-and-forthing the music of constellations!

That's just the beginning!

You see, such an extraordinary expanse of which Kai the tumbling little blue kite is only a tiny, tiny part means that others allways — as in all ways — have plenty of space!

And with that, Kai at last understands what it really means to do good on behalf of those he knows well, those he's just met, those he'll someday meet, and those he'll never meet, and even what it means to do good on behalf of those that time tells us are gone.

Good depends on granting others place.

And that requires courage.

And while he can't stop shaking with terror,

Kai still chooses to face

The Immense Monster Too Immense for Any One Name
and Hungrier Than All the Emptiness That Haunts
the Space Between All the Stars.

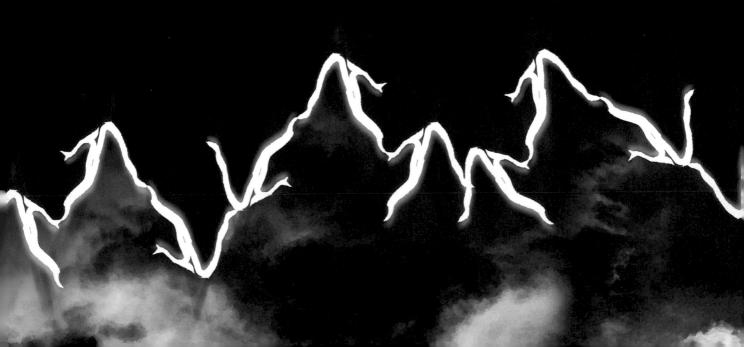

And then once and for all, Kai lets go of . . .

fear.

Guess what Kai the tumbling little blue kite lets go of next!

Tumbling!

Then what do you think Kai the little blue kite lets go of?

Blue!

After that, Kai the little kite lets go of little!

Then Kai the kite lets go of Kai!

Then the kite lets go of the kite!

And only light remains!

Until light is released too!

And then only darkness remains!

Until darkness is released and nothing reigns!

Until nothing is also freed . . .

Now, some say here was the end.

The Little Blue Kite was lost.

Kai was lost.

But, as it turns out, here is not the end . . .

Because, as it turns out, without anything there is still nothing **and** something. Because something to be that something needs nothing in the way. And nothing to be that nothing needs something to give away.

And, of course, as we all know, stars still shimmer and, well, moons still glow. Wild storms rant and warm breezes roam while spring's return keeps drawing new clearings into view. And maybe most important of all,

The Little Blue Kite still flies high above . . .

No thread needed . . .

Just Kai!

Free of the Murk! **Amazed and abounding in joy! Returning to his family!** With potted succulents, local honey, and a bright checkered tin of pistachios!

Kai!

At the weddings of his friends! He's now a teacher too! Showing his many new students how to fly little kites of their own!

Kai!

Returning again and again
in the same way that gentle thoughts keep returning again and again
to a sky forever welcoming all of us to fly.

ART

Regina M. Gonzales

&

Mark Z. Danielewski

THANK-YOUS

TO THE SMALLER ONES

Tycho and Zarina Gannon,

Simon Lovett Greene, Juniper Elfman Modine,

Micah Ross, and, of course, Dexi.

TO THE LARGER ONES

Emberly Modine, Louis Elfman, Yumna Siddiqi,

Todd Gannon, Lola Greene, David Ross, Bridget Fonda,

Danny Elfman, Rita Raley, and my brother Kye.

TO THE SKY SHARERS

Jackie Galerne, Michele Reverte, Jesse Simms, Peter Cagala, Justin Adair, Ryan Short, Daniel Williams, Hayley V. Brittania, Zack Warren, Jake Asher, Shauna Blake, Norbert Böhm, Josh Devine, g@rp, Michael Kirkham, Georgiy Malyshev, Shayan Mawlood, Larry McCaffery, Jessica Nelson, Anna Otto, Leslie Stewart, Dreebs Thornhill, Eleonora Todde, Kyle Vesely, Bryant Viegut, Alexander Weir, Kevin Williams, and Miles Woodfield.

TO THE BOOK DREAMERS

Edward Kastenmeier, Andy Hughes, Lydia Buechler,

Shona McCarthy, Mark Birkey, John Gall, and Altie Karper.

Circle Round A Stone Productions, Inc.

Atelier Z

No kites were hurt in the making of this book.